Clementine and Mungo

Sarah Dyer

BLOOMSBURY

This is Clementine and this is Mungo,
Clementine's younger brother.

Clementine knows a lot of things,
so Mungo is always asking her questions.

One sunny day Clementine and Mungo
went outside to play with the cat.

"Clementine," asked Mungo, "how do
cats stay cool in the summer?"

"Well, Mungo, when cats get
too hot they can take their
coats off," Clementine told him.

leaves are green,

"And, these trees,
why is it that some

and some are red?"
asked Mungo.

"Because, when it's time, tiny painting pig-ments go around and paint all the leaves from green to red," Clementine told him.

"And if we dig down here in the garden what will we find?" asked Mungo.

"Why the center of the earth of course!" replied Clementine.

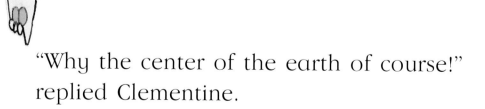

"we could start now if you li

heard it's not far," she said.

They did not get far and it was getting dark. Tired and muddy, they went home and Clementine helped Mungo get his bath ready.

"Clementine, why does water come out of the tap hot?" asked Mungo.

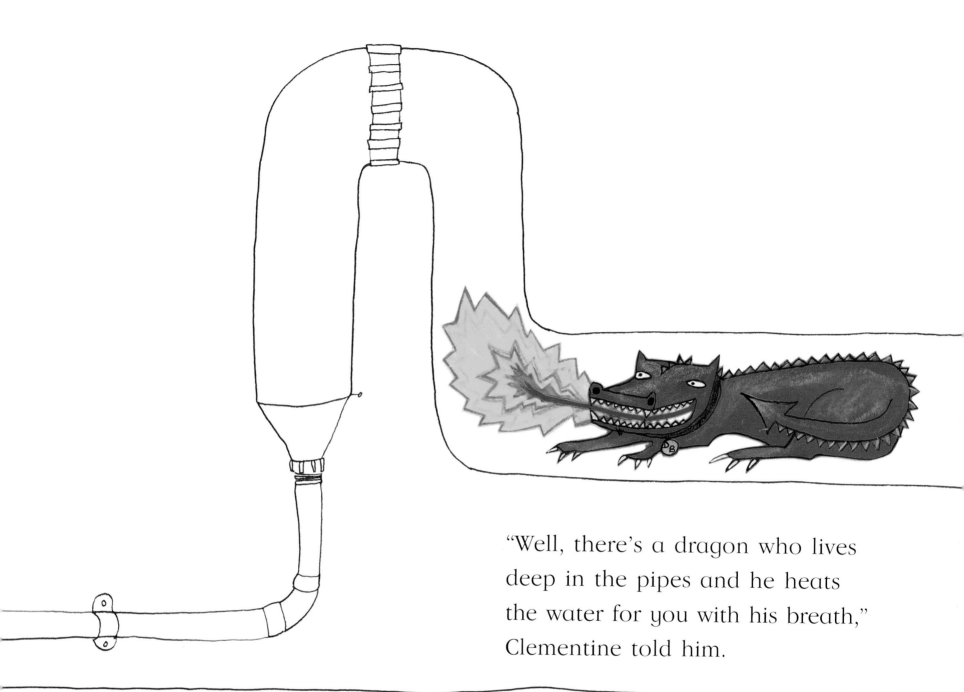

"Well, there's a dragon who lives
deep in the pipes and he heats
the water for you with his breath,"
Clementine told him.

After the nice bath Mungo was
ready for bed.
"Why don't we see the stars
in the daytime, Clementine?"
asked Mungo.

"Because at
night a
huge blanket
with star-
shaped holes
is pulled across
the sky,"
Clementine
told him.

After Mungo had admired the stars,

Clementine and Mungo cuddled up in bed.

Then Clementine asked Mungo a question.

"At night, when it gets very dark, why don't

you get scared, Mungo?" she whispered.

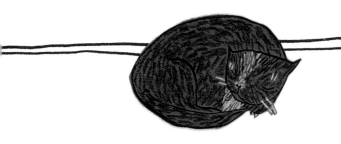

Mungo looked at Clementine, smiled, and
said, "because I know you are always there
for me, Clementine."
With that both Clementine and Mungo
curled up together dreaming of tomorrow.

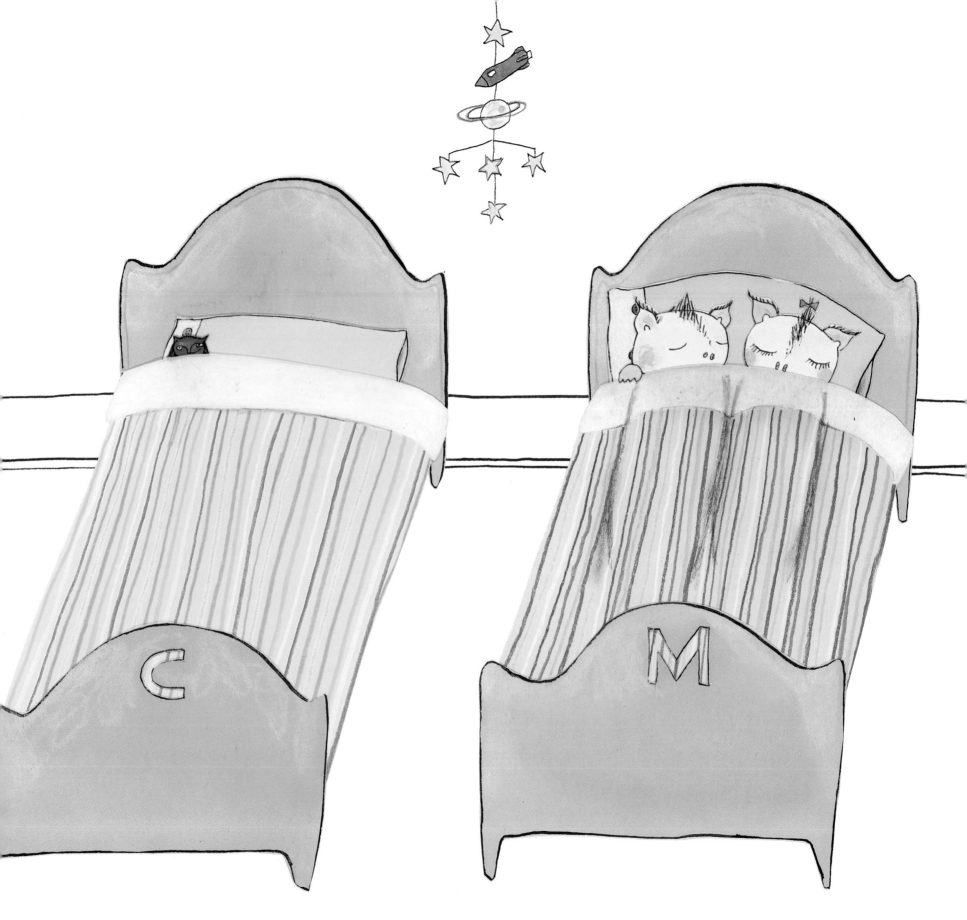

DATE DUE